For my dearest Claire,
who always asks
the most interesting questions…
And for her papa who made her possible.

www.mascotbooks.com

What Do You Believe, Mama?

For more information, please contact:
Mascot Books
560 Herndon Parkway #120
Herndon, VA 20170
info@mascotbooks.com

Library of Congress Control Number: 2016920545

CPSIA Code: PBANG0717A
ISBN-13: 978-1-63177-242-9

Printed in the United States

What Do You Believe, Mama?

written by Ann Bilodeau

illustrated by Stanley Burford

Many people believe in God,
because that is their tradition.

Different religions
have different traditions.

But some people say that
I am bad if I don't believe.

You don't have to believe in God to be good.

Are you good?

I try to be
a good HUMAN BEING—
just like people
who believe in God.

I believe in
caring for people with
RESPECT,
KINDNESS,
ACCEPTANCE,
FAIRNESS,
and LOVE.

I believe
in knowing
right from wrong
and making good choices.

But God created us
and the earth, right?

The earth is made of
STARDUST.

You are made of
STARDUST.

Should I believe in God?

DON'T LET ANYONE
TELL YOU WHAT TO BELIEVE.

Look for things that are true.
Be open to ideas.
Listen to your heart.

AND KEEP ASKING QUESTIONS!

You will know
what is right for you.

I WILL!

Remember,
I believe in YOU!

About the Author

Ann Burford Bilodeau

Growing up, I attended a Methodist church—mainly on the holidays and special occasions. This was our family tradition. I never felt connected to a higher being, but certainly appreciate the many moral lessons found in various religious ideologies. A common one is the idea of the golden rule, or to treat others as you would like to be treated. When I was given the gift of a beautiful and bright baby daughter in 2003, I wanted to find ways to teach her these important lessons—but from a secular perspective. Of course, reading has always been a joyful part of our lives, yet I could not find a book that shared my humanist thoughts. With the artistic gift of my treasured and dear aunt, Stanley Burford, my words and thoughts have come to life in this book. May you and your little one find joy in the message within!

The author is a graduate of Purdue University, a speech-language pathologist, and a clinical faculty member at Butler University. She is a member of the Center for Inquiry-Indiana and resides happily in Indianapolis with her husband Marc, daughter Claire, and their fat and fluffy cat Oreo.

About the Illustrator

Stanley Burford

The illustrator is a retired professor of art at the Herron School of Art and Design in Indianapolis, Indiana. She is now working daily in her studio in a peaceful, small forest on a large lake in North Carolina. Her work has been in over 200 exhibitions and one-woman shows around the country, winning numerous awards. Her work is also featured in over 280 private and corporate collections.